Charles F. A. Simonin

A Pedaller Abroad

Being an Illustrated Narrative of the Adventures and Experiences of a Cycling Twain

During a 1,000 kilomètre Ride in and Around Switzerland

Charles F. A. Simonin

A Pedaller Abroad
Being an Illustrated Narrative of the Adventures and Experiences of a Cycling Twain During a 1,000 kilomètre Ride in and Around Switzerland

ISBN/EAN: 9783337142223

Printed in Europe, USA, Canada, Australia, Japan

Cover: Foto ©Andreas Hilbeck / pixelio.de

More available books at **www.hansebooks.com**

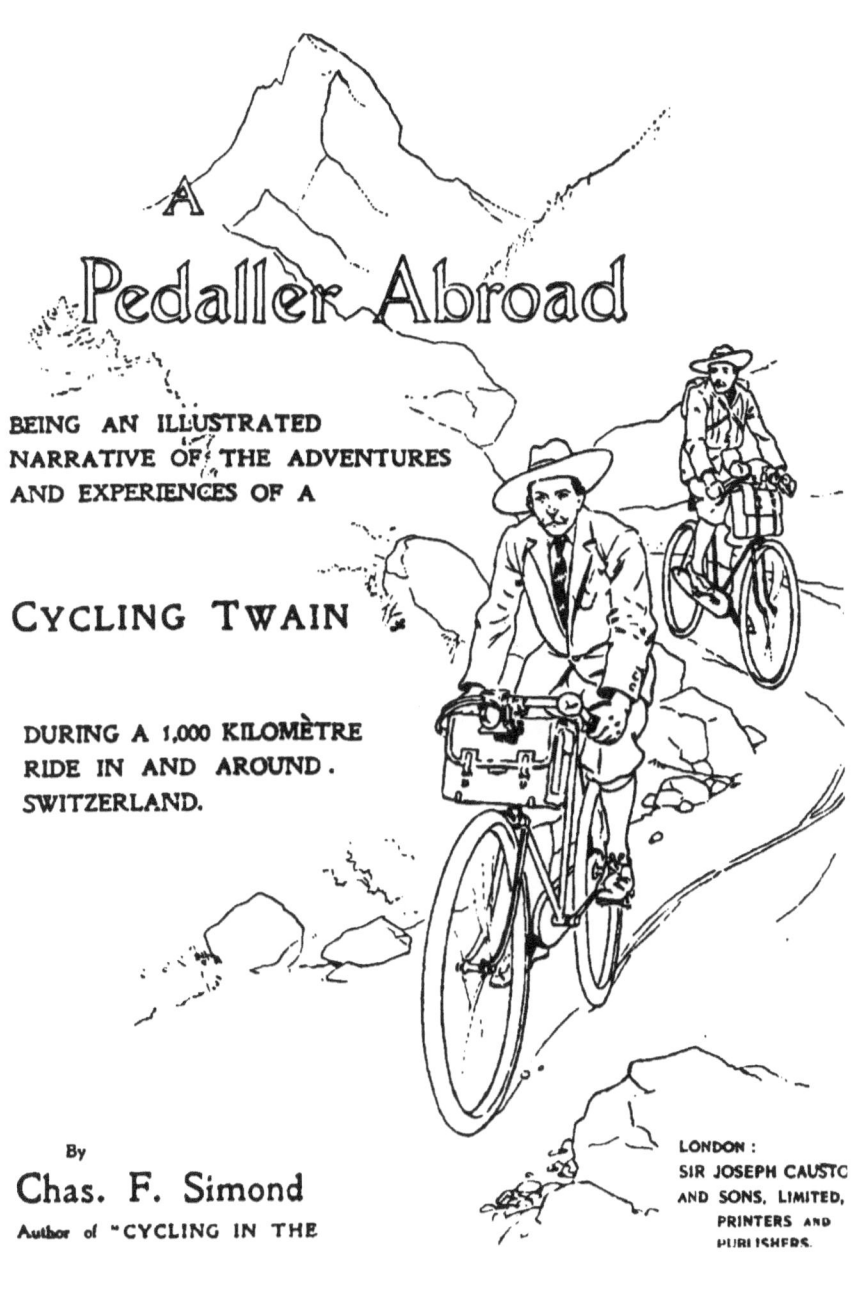

A Pedaller Abroad

BEING AN ILLUSTRATED
NARRATIVE OF THE ADVENTURES
AND EXPERIENCES OF A

CYCLING TWAIN

DURING A 1,000 KILOMÈTRE
RIDE IN AND AROUND .
SWITZERLAND.

By
Chas. F. Simond
Author of "CYCLING IN THE

LONDON :
SIR JOSEPH CAUSTO
AND SONS, LIMITED,
PRINTERS AND
PUBLISHERS.

A Pedaller Abroad.

*

CONTENTS.

PREFACE.

IN writing the following narrative I have attempted to give my impressions of a three weeks' holiday spent last summer on bicycles in and around Switzerland. It is at once a most enjoyable and inexpensive way of seeing that lovely country, which is not as yet overcrowded with cyclists.

During the tour I have described we were not favoured by the weather; but in spite of a superfluity of thunderstorms and generally unsettled conditions, we came back greatly benefited by the change, and delighted with our trip of 1896.

The illustrations which appear in this book are reproduced from photographs taken by my companion and self, and by Messrs. Ernesto Büchi, G. Sommer & Figlio, J. Tairraz, and the Photoglob Co., all well-known photographers of Switzerland and its environs. The map we used on this and many other rides was R. Leuzinger's "Nouvelle Carte de la Suisse," price Fcs. 6, mounted on linen and obtainable almost anywhere in Switzerland.

As regards a mount my advice is :—

BUY CYCLE HIGH GRADE TO
BICYCLE HIGH GRADIENTS.

THE AUTHOR.

Sir Joseph Causton & Sons,
Eastcheap, London E.C. Ltd.

Switzerland Revisited on a Bicycle.

Chapter I.

" DÉLÉMONT—Délémont. Les voyageurs pour Tavannes, Bienne, Berne et Neuchatel changent de train." These words, in the monotonous voice of a very sleepy porter at Délémont station, reminded us that, so far as the train was concerned, our journey was at an end. And we weren't sorry, my friend and I, after that hot night's journey across France. We had ridden a tandem bicycle from London to Dover, *via* Maidstone and Ashford, a few days before, but thinking a gear of 76 in. (which was the gear of our mount) too high, and the machine too light for the trip we were about to commence, we decided to send it back to town and trust to two singles which had been promised ready for us on our arrival in Switzerland. Result—we had to undergo that stuffy and generally uninteresting journey from Calais to Délémont, which is not so very many miles over the Franco-Swiss frontier, and from where we had determined to commence our annual tour on the Continent. I really think it worth while—and I speak from past experience of Continental cycling, for the most part in Switzerland, where I was one of the first riders (if not the actual pioneer) of safety bicycling—to take one's own mount over, and more especially if one is a member of the C.T.C. The French Railway Companies very rightly consider a cycle as luggage of the passenger, and a nominal fee of a penny is charged for registration, so that, always excepting the extortionate demand of 7s. 6d. for the carriage of a bicycle accompanied by the owner, and at his risk, from London to Calais or *vice versâ*, one has not much trouble with one's mount, and at the same time one knows its peculiarities and good or bad points. In our case, however, as before stated, we trusted to the machines secured beforehand on hire in Switzerland, and at the end of our ride we were so delighted with our mounts (full roadsters, and weighing 33 or 34 lbs.), that having the option to purchase them outright,

8

NEAR
YVERDON.

we decided to buy them. They were new machines at the time, and we were more than satisfied with the bargain, as bargain each machine was. But to this narrative.

My friend, who has accompanied me on many other similar and more or less enjoyable and exciting trips, is an artist whom I shall call X, which can stand for the unknown quantity of good (or bad) traits in his character.

For a really thorough change of living and scenery I recommend Switzerland to enthusiastic cyclists, who are fit and strong enough for hard up and down-hill work.

I have, at various times, been pretty well all through it, from the Jura to the Alps, and over the highest and most difficult passes.

Although in such a mountainous country one must naturally do a good deal of pushing, the engineering skill displayed in the Alpine Routes is so marvellous, one is able, by steady riding, to surmount many of them without undue fatigue, owing to the slight gradients of the winding roads in these parts.

It is needless to say a really good and reliable brake is absolutely essential to anyone who contemplates a trip in the higher Alps (see *Badminton Magazine* of June, 1896), and in fact during the following ride we each had affixed to the driving wheel a pneumatic brake, as well as the ordinary "plunger" pattern on the steering-wheel.

With the last-mentioned brake, as a safeguard for any special emergency, we found we could, with the greatest ease, govern the pace of our bicycles down the very steepest declines, and the elasticity of a resilient brake against a pneumatic tyre does not in the minutest degree injure the latter, whereas the pad of the former, when worn through after a certain amount of use, can easily be replaced, and with but a very small outlay. Another great safeguard against a runaway machine is a log of wood allowed to drag on the road some three or four yards behind the bicycle, and affixed to the saddle by a piece of string. This we found most useful in descending long unknown passes before we used the pneumatic brake. The idea has been most extensively copied, and very probably much improved upon. Be sure, reader, if you contemplate a trip in any of the lesser known parts of Switzerland, that you thoroughly understand your mount, as although in the larger towns you can most certainly get any small defect remedied, it is much more satisfactory to be able to repair any little accident that may occur to the machine, oneself.

VUITTEBOEUF,
NEAR YVERDON.

If you have a gear-case, have one that is easily detachable, as nothing is more annoying than not being able to get easily at the chain when one is almost certain that it is the cause of the trouble. Probably all this has been said many times before, but I am recounting my exact impression of cycling in Switzerland, and a more enjoyable way of seeing that most lovely of countries it is difficult to imagine. Walking, of course, is an excellent though slow mode of progression, and from a train you can't see on both sides, behind and in front. Of course, there is the ancient *diligence*, but as "the old order changeth, yielding place to new," I recommend a bicycle.

Chapter II.

WELL, having been informed that we had arrived at Délémont (1,430 ft.), we got out of the train and walked across the road from the station to the Hôtel de la Gare, just opposite. Here we hired a room for a change, clean up and rest, before we started on the first stage of our ride. Besides, we had to adjust the bicycles very carefully to insure comfortable riding, and we found the landlord, who happens to be a cyclist and speaks a little English, most obliging in helping us to fix on our carriers, etc.

Just before starting, I remember asking a German-Swiss the French for "gear-case," and for some time could not make him understand what part of the machine I meant; but at last he said, with a strong German accent, "Oh, fous foulez tire un cartère." I afterwards found out he was under the impression this was the translation for a gear-case, but he had got mixed up with the well-known maker's name, viz., "Carter." The correct French is, I believe, "garde-châine."

I accounted for the camera and "surgery," besides a valise, on a carrier in front, and by

VUITTEBOEUF,
NEAR
YVERDON.

17

the time the bicycles had " all on," we nicknamed them the " Christmas trees." The
camera in question was a No. 2 Frena, containing 40 films, and although this naturally
adds considerably to the weight carried, it is
so convenient to be able to " snap off " a
pretty bit of scenery or amusing incident on

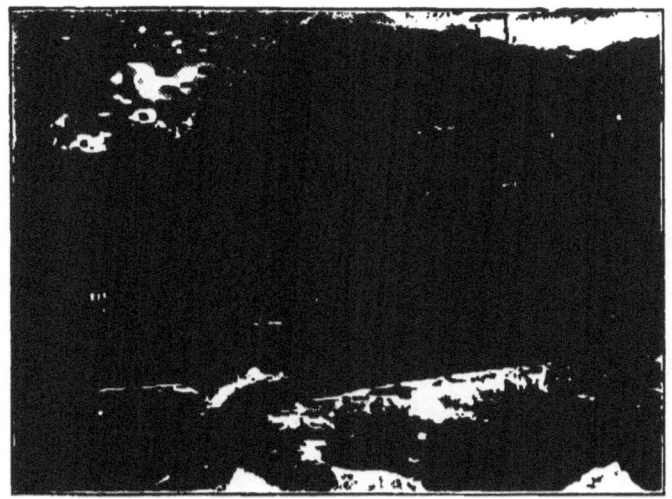

MÜNSTER THAL.

the day's run, and gives great pleasure on
one's return, especially during the process of
development and printing.

At last we were ready with the carriers,
horns, lanterns, pneumatic brakes, etc., all
securely fixed on, and started after a good
breakfast, about ten o'clock, on a muggy damp

morning in June, *en route* for Bienne, *viâ* the Münster Thal. Of course we rode somewhat gingerly at first, so as to get our rather shaken muscles into playing order, but warming to our work, we soon got over a half-dozen miles of not very attractive scenery before entering the Münster Thal at Courrendlin. By the way, we soon found out that those horns, the Swiss

MÜNSTER THAL.

seem so fond of putting on their bicycles, are absolutely inefficient for warning purposes, even a small way ahead, and I suggest the loudest gong or bell procurable.

SENTIER DES VEAUX,
NEAR
YVERDON.

21

Later on we made use of small blowing-horns, which, though very effectual for the purpose used, are not always immediately at hand in an emergency. The Münster Thal, or Val Moutier, watered by the Birs river, is a wild and rugged ravine, composed for the most part of huge limestone rocks, and the railway line from Courrendlin is carried through these by means of cuttings, tunnels and galleries, and in fact follows the road to Roche (1,650 ft.), soon after which travellers by train must content themselves with scraps of the bewitching scenery, seen as they thread their way through nine short tunnels after passing through one of 100 yards.

Soon after we had taken one or two photos, we reached Moutier (1,730 ft.), a sweetly situated and thriving village on the left bank of the river Birs. Finding the weather very oppressive we rested a little here, and at the Café de Jura refreshed the inner man, the while admiring (?) the very terrible pictures that adorned the walls of the " Gaststube." We always called these rooms " gas tubes," because of the amount of brag the peasants indulge in, under the influence of " un verre." One painting represented several chamois hunters being butted by their would-be quarry, and one unfortunate going headlong down an abyss while the animal prepares to send another hunter after the first. Then on another wall was the picture of a daring mountaineer essaying to rob an elderly lady eagle of her young. She naturally resents this intrusion, and by the look of anguish on the man's face and the state of his clothes, he must have had an exceedingly *mauvais quart d'heure* previous to the artist's arrival on the scene. After gazing in awe at several other equally peerless works of art, we thought we'd better move on, which we accordingly did, a crowd of admiring peasants seeing us off on our journey to Mérilay for our first *déjeuner à la fourchette* in Switzerland. Here rain delayed us rather longer than we liked, as the inn wasn't over comfortable, and there was nothing interesting in the village itself. At length we continued the even tenor of our way, the excellent road threading through the grassy meadows round Sorvilier, Bévilard and Reconvillier to Tavannes (2,500 ft.), a large village close to the source of the Birs river. Here we had to dismount and push our bicycles up to the " Pierre Pertuis," which consists of a gap in the rock through which the road passes. This used to be fortified in

LAUSANNE.

25

the Roman times, and is quite a natural aperture. The letters and figures on the keystone as it were, of the arch were too worn to be legible, but looking back through this opening we had a very pretty view of Tavannes and the Münster Thal for some distance. Remounting at the top we found a rather too steep descent to Sonceboz (2,150 ft.), although with our pneumatic brakes we were able to negotiate it in safety.

Sonceboz is the junction for the railway to La Chaux-de-Fonds, an important watch-making town, and as the history of the introduction of the first watch to this town about the end of the 17th century is some-what interesting, I shall give it as it was told me.

A cattle dealer was the proud possessor of the wonder, which naturally created a vast amount of excitement among the simple herdsmen and charcoal burners ; till one day it stopped, to the great dismay of the entire population. Dansel Jean Richard, a young man of an enquiring nature, took upon himself to take the marvellous piece of mechanism to pieces, and what was more, succeeded in putting them together again, and gave it a new lease of life. He was not satisfied till he had made a watch for himself, and, after a hundred trials and disappointments, at last met with success, and became the father of what is now a most important manufacture.

The road now followed the Suze or Schüss river down stream. There are some lovely bits of scenery on all sides, with numerous cascades and waterfalls, which were in all their splendour after so much rain. It is a lovely wooded valley here, which suddenly contracts, and we entered the narrow passage that the river has forced through the Jura range, and soon after espied Bienne below us to the south, with the whole chain of Alps far away to Mont Blanc—a very striking view after the darkness of the ravine, and seen splendidly from close to where the train emerges from a tunnel near a lofty bridge.

We soon after arrived at Bienne, where, it being about 4.30, we repaired to a confectioner's near the station for tea. I don't know the name of the shop, but in case any sweet-toothed cyclist passes through this town, I recommend him or her to sample some of their *petits fours* and ices, previous to looking over an interesting collection of Celtic and Roman antiquities to be seen at the Museum Schwab.

Bienne, or Biel (1,445 ft.), is a very ancient

town, and as there are several nice hotels round the station, it makes a good halting place. However, we decided to ride on along the lake of Bienne to Neuchatel for the night.

All the way from Bienne to Neuveville and thence to Neuchatel, there is a magnificent road close to the waters of the lakes of Bienne and Neuchatel. One has a very pleasing view of both lakes, backed by the superb chain of Bernese Alps. German was the native tongue chiefly spoken up to Neuveville on our ride, but at this town the French language took its place. Some little time before we reached the lake of Neuchatel (25 miles long and 4 or 5 broad) we took a snap-shot of peasants drinking their beer and discussing their neighbours in general, and us and our bicycles in particular, but I'm sorry to say the plate was even more fogged than the peasants by the time they had imbibed their fill.

Neuchatel (1,433 ft.) is a large town beautifully located on the lake at the base of the Jura mountains. The town abounds in fine buildings, the handsome Post Office being among the most noticeable. We put up at the Hôtel Bellevue opposite it, and situated near the small harbour—very comfortable indeed, but rather expensive.

Chapter III.

THERE is a lot to be seen at Neuchatel, including a collection of paintings by Swiss artists, while the market place and Place Purry are also worth a visit.

Heavy rain during the night and most of the next day, but as we had determined to push on to the other end of the lake, where the small and ancient town of Yverdon is situated, we braved the elements and started off in capes and caps for a muddy ride. We had both ridden these 26 miles many times, so knew the route well. Though there are several hills, which are more comfortable to walk than ride, the surface of the roads is excellent and the scenery charming. The small villages dotted about on the vine-clad and grassy slopes of the Jura make a very pretty picture, and I'm sure if this part of Switzerland were better known to the general run of tourists, they would be delighted with the many exquisite spots round about. For instance, the Gorges de l' Areuse, close to Auvernier (through which we passed), are the very prettiest gorges one could wish to see, although of

SAILING BARGE
ON LAC LÉMAN.

late years, owing to extensive works to utilize the water power at Neuchatel, they have lost some of their wild beauty. A walk up to the Champs du Moulin, and thence on to

GORGES DE L'AREUSE.

Noiraigue and the Creux du Vent, was one of our favourite excursions years ago ; the latter place being an excellent point of vantage from which to witness that glorious sight in Switzerland — the sunrise. From Auvernier we rode on through to Concise (1,453 ft.), where the thunderstorm that had been threatening for some time burst over us. We let it pass off before remounting our machines and riding through Grandson, noted for its pretty old château, under an arch of which the train passes on its way to Yverdon. The "Château de Grandson" is said to date from the year 1000, and has been the scene of several battles,

YVERDON.

the principal one between the Swiss and Burgandese, when the latter were defeated. Just as you enter Yverdon by road from Grandson you pass the racecourse. By the irony of fate this racecourse was made over the graves of hundreds and thousands of horses that had to be shot for want of fodder, after the entry of Bourbaki's army into Switzerland in 1871. By the way, another charming gorge (through which some of this army marched) is situated about ten miles from Yverdon, and called

"Le Sentier de Covattanaz." It begins at a village at the foot of the Jura, Vuittebœuf by name, and goes through a pretty defile up to Ste. Croix, a village famous for the manufacture of watches and musical boxes.

In the time of solid tyres we used to push

PESTALOZZI STATUE.

our bicycles up the Sentier (and an arduous task it was), and then coast down the long gradual descents of the high road which zigzags on the mountain side, pulling ourselves up, by the aid of powerful brakes, at the sharp bends in the road. There were no thoughts then of tyres puncturing or bursting, and many a rush down an almost impossible hill have I enjoyed, mounted on one of the first safeties that ever found its way to Switzerland—a No. 1 Rudge with solid tyres. Well, we had arrived at Yverdon more or less wet through, and stayed a few nights with friends. It is an

CHEYRES, NEAR YVERDON.

interesting town enough, but I don't recommend a protracted stay in it, although a week or so spent at " Les Bains," charmingly situated about half a mile from the town, would give one a chance of seeing some of the very prettiest

WASHERWOMEN AT YVONAND.

country in this so slightly known part of " La Belle Suisse."

Please let it be known I don't mention the names of the various hotels or inns we put up at for advertising purposes, but merely as a guide to any cyclists or others who may contemplate a ride such as I am describing. At Yverdon, by the way, there is a thoroughly competent bicycle maker and repairer—Meyer by name—who is well known (at least on the Continent) for his long-distance road riding, and understands his business in all its details. A new *piste*, or cycle track, has lately been laid down at this small and enterprising town, where several meetings are held during the season under the auspices of the flourishing "Cycliste Club d'Yverdon." There is also a castle to visit, and a fine bronze statue of Pestalozzi (the pedagogue) on the market place, where it was erected some few years ago. A museum of antiquities completes the list of objects of interest to be seen in the town, and has lately become possessed of an Egyptian mummy, supposed to be over 2,000 years old. Rather a good tale is told of the gentleman who brought it over as a present to the museum. On arriving at Marseilles, the porter was entirely at a loss to know under what style of luggage or merchandise to classify it for registration, but seemed to be quite satisfied when the owner exclaimed, "Oh! call it fresh meat."

Chapter IV.

WE passed out of Yverdon by the afore-mentioned "Les Bains," and kept along the valley, which is dotted with an old castle here and there, and with small scattered villages, till a gradual ascent brought us to Echallens. Light railways seem to follow all the chief roads, and the casual way the children and cattle stray on and off the lines is ludicrous to a degree. We got an enchanting view of Mont Blanc and the Lake of Geneva some half-hour before we descended through Lausanne to Ouchy, from where we had agreed to take the steamer.

Lac Léman, as the Vaudois prefer it called the most beautiful of the western lakes of Switzerland, can be most appreciated from the steamer. Is it not Byron who says :—

> "Lake Léman woos him with its crystal face,
>   The mirror where the stars and mountains view
>   The stillness of their aspect in each trace,
>   Its clear depths of their far height and blue."

There is such a combination here of sublimity and grandeur, mingled with softness and beauty ; the massive Alps of the Savoy forming the southern horizon, with a foreground of green pastures and of darker green forests interspersed with châlets and small houses. It is indeed a lovely spot, and it seemed very pleasant to

COWS LEAVING YVERDON FOR THE MOUNTAINS.

loll on the deck of the steamer " Winkelried," which bore us swiftly and smoothly down the lake to Geneva, and on board of which we met such an amusing American, that what with his yarns and funny expressions, the time passed only too quickly, and we found ourselves at this well deservedly favourite resort, which this year was full to overflowing, of tourists visiting its pretty exhibition. However, as one exhibition is so like another, we contented ourselves with a very cursory glance round it, though lingering some while to admire the model Swiss village, which is certainly most interesting, beautifully arranged and put together. As I hear an English company has purchased the entire village with a view to

STEAMER REACHING OUCHY QUAY.

transporting it to England, we shall, no doubt, have an opportunity of seeing it at one of our London exhibitions.

At Geneva (1,243 ft.) there are so many first-class hotels, it is hardly worth while mentioning we stayed for the night at the Hôtel de l'Europe, which we found exceedingly comfort-able, central and clean.

How we blessed the natives next morning when we were doing our level best to get out of the town on our way to Chamonix *viâ* Cluses! Everyone we asked seemed to have a different opinion as to the right road for leaving Geneva, and at last, exasperated at the seeming ignorance of our informants, we struck out our own route by the map, and fortunately hit the right one.

It is altogether about 60 miles to Chamonix, a good road all the way, and unless one stays the night at St. Gervais, I recommend cyclists to try and get through in the day, for at Sallanches, where we stayed the night, we were most uncomfortable ; so for obvious reasons I shall not mention the name of the hostelry which sheltered us.

We rode out of Geneva by Annemasse (1,420 ft.), where a tram-line we had decided on following ends, and shortly after had a most magnificent view of Mont Blanc in the distance, on our left.

> " Far, far above, piercing the infinite sky,
> Mont Blanc appears still snowy and serene."

This valley is very lovely, and all the way to Bonneville we admired its meadows and gardens, its orchards and forests, while here and there appeared châteaux and large villas

PONT DE STE. MARIE,
AND MONT BLANC.

From a Photo by J. Tairraz.

to enhance the beauty of the scene. It is called the Arve Valley, after the river which waters it and which we crossed when leaving Bonneville. By the bye, we were then in the Haute Savoie, having crossed the boundary at Foron, and how quickly one notices the long stretches of road directly one gets into France! For a pedestrian they must seem very tedious, straight as a die for mile after mile, but on the faithful wheel one spins along at a grand rate on the perfect metal, and in this way we got through to Bonneville for our first halt and rest in excellent time.

This town is very attractively placed among vine-clad hills, and boasts a monument, on the west side of a fine bridge across the Arve, dedicated to the Savoyards who fell in the campaign of 1870-1. Another superb view of Mont Blanc gladdened our eyes as we started along the left bank of the river for Cluses (1,605 ft.) in almost a straight line. On arriving at the Hôtel National there, and enquiring the hour of day, we found we had actually done the last eight or nine miles in literally no time, as of course, being in France, the clock was fifty-five minutes slower than the Swiss or Central European time. We had, therefore, an extra rest there. A charming

French Phyllis, with a milk and roses complexion and in a blue cotton dress, administered to our wants. We had *thé complet*, and on one of the plates (which I should much have liked to take with me but for the bother of carrying it and the chances of a tumble), there was a scene entitled " Divorce," representing a typical French *paysan* as central figure, together with the various adjuncts to a court of law. The following dialogue explains the picture :—

JUGE : Pourquoi voulez-vous divorcer?

PAYSAN : Ma femme est trop vieille j'peux pus avoir d'amis.

Being a somewhat novel plea, I thought it worth while recording.

At present the railway to Chamonix terminates at Cluses, but the completion of the line to Sallanches is being rapidly pushed on by gangs of Italian workmen, who one and all seemed willing to respond gaily to our " Buongiorno," although it was rather late in the day to make that remark.

CHAMONIX.

Chapter V.

AND so on to Sallanches, where, as before mentioned, we passed a very uncomfortable night. Owing to some expedition organised by the Continental Time Table Society having

NEAR SALLANCHES.

secured most of the food in the place, we had great difficulty in getting a square meal, although we were ravenous after a good steady ride, slightly ascending all the day. And then when we retired to bed, longing to sink into the arms of Morpheus, we only succeeded in courting "more fleas." In spite of these unpleasant bed-fellows we slept fairly well, except for a serenade from two Frenchmen, who had evidently dined not wisely but too well, and kept up a sort of loud chant in the room adjoining ours for most of the night, as it seemed to us. One thing well repaid our halt here, and that was the sun setting on Mont Blanc, which gave us the opportunity of witnessing once again, in all its parti-coloured beauty, the "Alpine Glow," or *Alpen-glühen*. There is only one thing to equal a sunset, and that is a sunrise, and after seeing both at their best, I cannot determine which shall receive the palm. One gets an admirable survey of this giant of mountains from Sallanches, and magnificent he looked bathed in the many tints of the sunset opposite his majesty, and later on in all his grandeur as the moon cast her white rays full on the enormous mass of dazzling snow and diaphanous ice. Truly a noble and sublime spectacle!

All the way up from Geneva there are cascades in abundance, and most of them were very imposing after so much rain. Naturally we left Sallanches without much regret, passing

MER DE GLACE,
CHAMONIX.

51

shortly afterwards close to St. Gervais-les-Bains and Le Fayet (1,860 ft.), and then ascending gradually went through a cutting and entered the wooded valley of "Le Châtelard." Just as one leaves this cutting, the Dôme du Gouter and Aiguille du Midi appear in the distance.

Almost immediately after comes a short tunnel, the scenery all the while being exquisite and more alpine at every mile. Then crossing the Arve by the Pont Ste. Marie, the glaciers gradually came into sight, the first being those of "de Griaz" and "de Taconnay," and further on "des Bossons."

Then riding through a village of the same name we came into Chamonix, nestling at the foot of Mont Blanc, which was beginning to be clouded over near the summit; and we were informed by the weather-wise that this betokened a storm.

They were quite correct in their prognostications, as we had a severe thunder and hail storm during the following night.

At the Hôtel d'Angleterre we found ourselves very comfortable during our stay; but what can I say that has not already been written of Chamonix? Of course we visited the "Mer de Glace"—a most appropriate name, as seen from above it certainly does resemble a huge frozen angry sea.

From a guide book to Chamonix, given to me by the proprietor of the Hôtel d'Angleterre,

TAKEN AT TÊTE NOIRE.

I take the following anecdote, *à propos* of the inauguration day of the cabane on the "Grands Mulets" in 1850, when fifty persons lodged the night in this shelter-house of 14 ft. long by 6½ ft. broad, heated by a stove and lighted by two windows.

ARGENTIÈRE.

From a Photo by the Photoglob Co

55

" First of all the table and benches were taken out," says Mr. M. C. Durier, in his interesting work on Mont Blanc, "then the most distinguished members of the company sat down

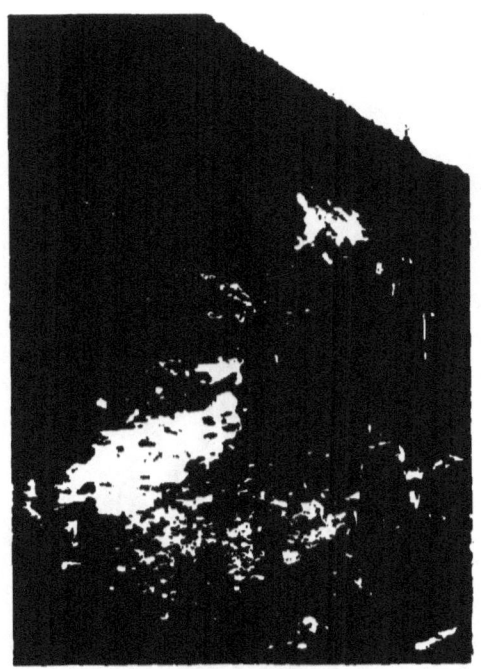

TÊTE NOIRE PASS.

on the floor with their backs to the wall; a second file took its place between their legs, and so it went on till the place was full. The last had a little difficulty in closing the door, and some squeezing was necessary before all could find a place. The door and the windows were now closed, and some one succeeded in putting some green wood into the stove; fifty pipes were now lighted simultaneously, and the utmost gaiety prevailed, when suddenly general

TÊTE NOIRE PASS.

suffocation was threatened, and all eyes were filled with tears. The stove failed to draw properly, and the smoke from the green wood was mingling with that from the pipes. The

ROCHE PERCÉE,
TÊTE NOIRE.

From a Photo by J. Tairraz.

guides alone were at their ease in this atmosphere; they were warm! Only when some one threatened to break the windows did they consent to let in a little fresh air, after which the festivities recommenced."

Since this episode another cabane has been

TRIENT.

built (just below the older one), of 52 ft. in length, and the surprise of the tourist when he finds so comfortable a lodging at such a height in the midst of icy wastes is difficult to describe.

Chamonix is more the centre for climbers than cyclists, and we had quite a little crowd of English people to start us on our ride over

TRIENT.

the Tête Noire Pass to Martigny. Although it is rideable to Argentière, and on certain parts of the Pass, there is a great deal of extremely hard work to be done in the walking and

From a Photo by J. Tairraz.

TÊTE NOIRE, AND
LES FINHAUTS.

pushing line, so beware of carrying any un-
necessary baggage on your machine over this
Pass, but send it on by *diligence* to Martigny,
or at least to the Tête Noire or Col de Forclaz
(the highest point of the Pass).

Soon after leaving Argentière and its huge
glacier, which descends between the Aiguille
Verte and the Aiguille du Chardonnet, we began
to ascend in long windings, and had a magnificent retrospective view of the first-named
mountain and the Glacier du Tour from Tréle-
champ. After crossing the Col des Montets
4,740 ft.) we could remount and descend
gradually into a wild ravine.

The "Cascade à Bérard," viewed from the
road, is very picturesque, but I am informed
it is well worth a closer inspection.

We did not, however, make this digression,
but pushed on through the lonely valley to
Vallorcine, and had a final survey of Mont
Blanc.

Thence the valley contracts with numerous
waterfalls on either side, and we crossed the
bridge (3,684 ft.) which is the boundary
between France and Switzerland. Being
plombés, we had no difficulty in passing our
bicycles through the Swiss douane, and leaving
the "Mauvais pas" route on our left, we had

about the stiffest climb imaginable to the Tête Noire or La Roche-Percée, up a very rough and narrow road.   From a wooden belvedere

GOATS AT MARTIGNY.

one has the most magnificent view in both directions of the superb gorge of the Eau-Noire.

The inn, though somewhat expensive, is very cosy and clean, and an excellent meal was soon forthcoming during our halt here.

A photo we took shows the way some cyclists

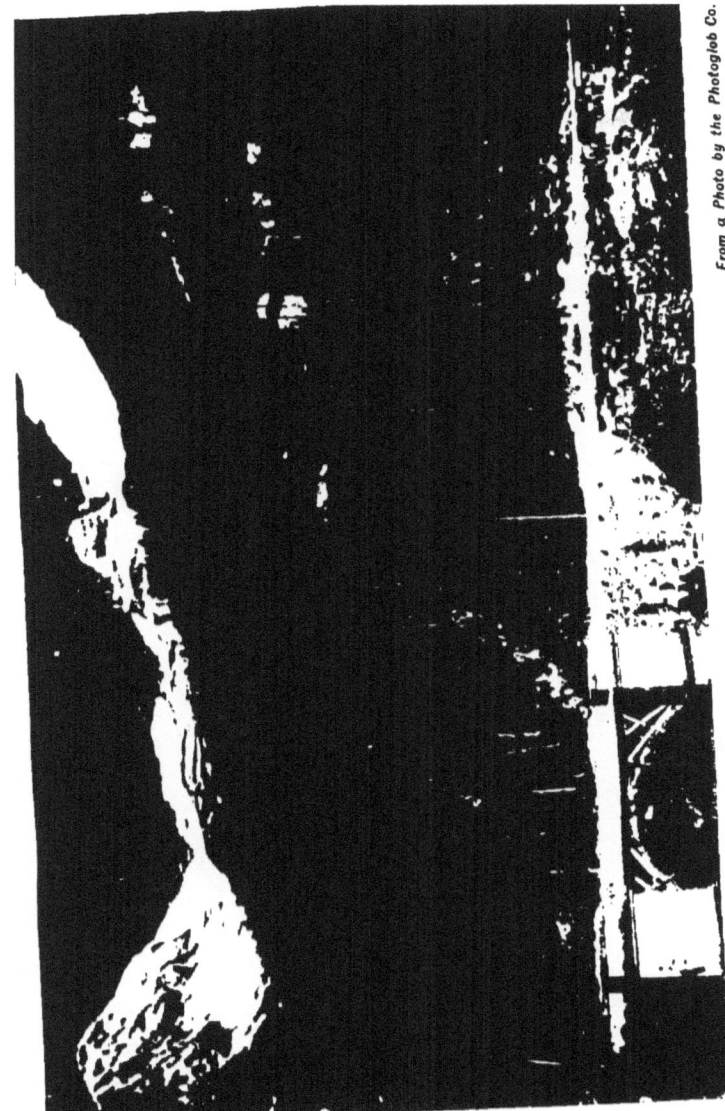

From a Photo by the Photoglob Co.

BÉRISAL AND
GANTER BRIDGE.

C 2

prefer to get their mounts up to Tête Noire, and certainly the road is not inviting for riding or pushing. We now continued along the Valley of Trient, through a not over dense forest of pine trees, and soon reached the village of the same name (4,250 ft.).

Here we found a very steep ascent to the Col de Trient or Col de la Forclaz (4,997 ft.), where we rested after the tiring push up the zigzag road from Trient. Now began the most precipitous descent I have ever negotiated on a bicycle, and we had to be very careful, even with the two brakes, especially rounding the sharp bends at the ends of each zigzag. And so we rode very quietly for 35 minutes or so downhill, when suddenly a magnificent landscape of the Rhone Valley, right away to Sion, with Martigny just below, opened out to our admiring eyes, and we reached the town without mishap, about an hour later.

At the Hôtel National in Martigny-ville (1,560 ft.) we were well looked after, but beyond being the starting place for the Great St. Bernard Pass as well as the one over which we had just come, the town isn't at all interesting, and there is very little to be seen there.

Chapter VI.

FROM Martigny to Riddes a route of about
ten miles goes as straight as an arrow, and
with a strong wind (such as one gets in the
Rhone Valley) behind us we soon rattled
these off, and rode on through various small
and listless villages to Sion (1,710 ft.) What
struck us most in the scenery from Martigny

SION.

was the plenitude of old castles on either side
of the valley, and of which a fair average
proudly retain their walls and towers in good
condition, in spite of the ravages of time and

From a Photo by G. Sommer & Figlio.

SIMPLON
ROAD.

the wars of the 13th century between "suzerain et vassal."

Of Martigny Castle only one tower remains in fairly good preservation, but as we reached Sion, its two old châteaux, " de Tourbillon" and "de Valère," on conical mounts, became prominent features in a really pretty landscape.

Besides these there is a small tower, called vulgarly the " Tour des Sorciers," probably because it is all that remains of ramparts which once surrounded a prison for wretches accused of sorcery, of which there were many in the 15th and 16th centuries.

Continuing to rise slightly, the road now brought us through several small attractive villages to the prettiest of them all, Sierre (1,765 ft.), where we stayed the night at the Hôtel Bellevue, which is an hotel I can most strongly recommend. The proprietors both speak English perfectly, and seem to take the keenest interest in seeing that their visitors are made as comfortable as possible.

Sierre has become during the last few years a most charming winter as well as a summer resort, and certainly its situation excels all other places in the Rhone Valley, while the comforts of the Belle Vue Hotel, which building has been greatly enlarged, are particularly adapted to the requirements of English visitors. In the summer, more especially, it is a well-known' resting-place for travellers going east or west.

A very useful and interesting little book entitled " Sierre and Montana," can be obtained at the hotel, and was principally written for the

HOTEL 'BELLE VUE, :SIERRE.

benefit of the yearly increasing number of English visitors who winter in this picturesque and beautiful spot in the midst of the Bernese and Valaisian Alps.

Besides the hotel, which is a dear old place, well poised on a hill, amidst abundant foliage, Sierre itself is a most interesting village, with many mediæval houses in various stages

74

of preservation. Old Sierre (Alt Sieders) is near Sierre on the south-west, and a tower in ruins close to the railway marks the place. The " Tour Goubin," or " Goubing Turm," dates back as far as 1297. Besides this, which belonged latterly to the De Courten family, there is one called " La Cour," also their property, but more modern in structure, having been erected in 1673 by Jean François de Courten, captain of the Gardes-Suisses in France. Antoine de Courten, an ancestor, and one of the partisans of the famous Supersaxo, died in the battle of " la Bicogne."

All the way up the Rhone Valley we particularly noticed the great number of mules used as beasts of draught. N.B.—They don't seem to like bicycles.

On the north the gentle slopes of the vineyards, which gradually lose themselves in the range of Bernese Alps, gives one the impression that the country round about Sierre is open, and this effect is greatly enhanced by the manner in which the plateau of the valley itself is broken by monticles of varying sizes and appearance, some being quite bare and arid, several capped with castles, and others covered with small firs and oaks. To antiquarians Sierre lends itself more especially, as it dates back as Sirrum, 517 A.D., and to them it is becoming more popular each year.

Several of its old castles have a reputation for being haunted, but if they are, no spooks disturbed our rest, and we started off next morning in the strongest wind I have ever ridden against.

The worst of it was, in spite of the wind in the valley being favorable for fine weather, high above, the clouds were moving slowly in a direction and manner that betokened rain, and . sure enough, after being blown to a standstill several times, as we reached Louèche, or Leuk, down came the rain in torrents, and although we waited a while here, we finished up at Brigue in a drenching storm, against which so-called mackintosh capes were as muslin. At Louèche (2,045 ft.) we found it very difficult to obtain interesting notes, but any not too exacting tourist could not fail to be charmed with the scenery alone. Here, too, is the beginning of the Gemmi Pass, but we continued our way through Turtmann to Visp, a picturesque village at the mouth of the Visp Valley, up which the railway goes to Zermatt.

We weren't sorry to get to Brigue (2,245 ft.), where we found a welcome shelter at the railway restaurant, to wait in vain for the rain to cease. Another fine castle here, called the " Stockalper Château," is the largest private residence in Switzerland. The man who built it (Kasper Stockalper by name) dominated the trade over the Simplon Pass, which he protected by a guard of seventy men. One should get fine views here of the Wassenhorn, Belalp, and Eggishorn.

Chapter VII.

As the weather seemed unwilling to ameliorate, we at last decided to push on (in both senses of the word) to Bérisal, nine miles from Brigue, and three parts of the way to the summit of the Simplon Pass. What a magnificent route it is to be sure, and how skilfully engineered!

Constructed by order of Napoleon I. in 1800-6, it was the first great Alpine route after the Brenner, and although the construction of the road, which is kept open all the year, is less striking than the Splügen and Schyn Passes, in my opinion the scenery is certainly as fine, if not more so.

From the post-office at Brigue, where the ascent begins, we had to push our machines up roads, which (although very good, no doubt in dry weather) were horribly muddy on our visit, nearly all the nine miles to Bérisal, except for a short spin when we were nearing our destination. As the route winds up over the green pastures, we had a finer and more imposing view of the Rhone Valley, and a glimpse of the Kaltwasser Glacier on the left,

From a Photo by G. Sommer & Figlio.

SIMPLON ROAD.
WINTER GALLERY.

which we were to pass on the morrow. At
the First Refuge (3,200 ft.) the road turned
sharply back, and we ascended the wooded
slope in many zigzags, and had even grander
surveys of the Rhone Valley and mountains
of the Aletsch region.

DILIGENCE.

Still ascending gradually, we passed the
diligences going to Brigue, and by the manner
their occupants were wrapped up we imagined
they must have had an uncommonly cold and
unpleasant drive. At the Second Refuge
(4,330 ft.) the Pass proper first comes into
sight, and it was just before crossing the
Ganter Bridge (4,820 ft.) that we were able
to ride for a mile or so (in liquid mire). The

Third Refuge, at an altitude of over 5,000 ft., seemed quite close from here, but it took us a good half-hour before we arrived at Bérisal, finely situated. The Hôtel de la Poste was well filled with visitors, but we managed to secure a very comfortable room and a hot bath, which we thought about the best precaution against a chill after our double drenching during this decidedly dirty day. Although rather an alliterative sentence, it about describes the state of affairs.

Our hostess, who was standing on the hotel steps, seemed to be rather surprised—nay, embarrassed—on my addressing her by her Christian name, as we had never had the pleasure of a previous meeting. A mutual friend at Sierre had told me how the lady in question was generally known, and the chance of gladdening our somewhat dampened spirits at the sight of the perplexed look which o'erspread her countenance on being hailed in such a friendly fashion by a total stranger, was too good to be missed, so I availed myself of it with great glee. They looked after us right royally at this little inn, and after supper, over an excellent cup of coffee, we recounted to them our adventures in a sort of Anglo-German-Italian-French language, and gave them an

From a Photo by G. Sommer & Figlio.

SIMPLON HOSPICE.

85

outline of our projected trip, with the result that although we started *de très bonne heure le lendemain*, we had quite an enthusiastic crowd to see us "fix up" the Christmas trees and wish us "Bon voyage."

Thank goodness! it had rained itself out in the night, and the roads had dried up very fairly (as it was their wont, when the sun, not to be outdone by the cyclists, comes out for a "scorching"), so that we got on well to the Fourth Refuge (5,645 ft.), from where we once more saw the top of the Pass. There was a great deal of snow on the sides of the road, though melting very quickly under the sun's rays. After passing through the "Kapflock," hewn in the rock for 100 ft., we came to the Fifth Refuge at an altitude of 6,345 ft. Then first under the Kaltwasser Glacier by the Wasser Gallery, the road passes through the Old Gallery and the longer Joseph Gallery (all containing, more or less, large amounts of snow and ice), and emerges at the Sixth Refuge (6,540 ft.), where we bid farewell to the view of the Bernese Alps, after a long gaze at these snow-capped giants.

Soon after, at the Col du Simplon, which is almost the top of the Pass, we reached the highest point of the route at an altitude above

sea-level of about 6,600 ft., after a stiffish climb
from Bérisal of over six miles. About five
minutes further on we came to the Simplon
Hospice (at the base of the Schönhorn), founded
by Napoleon, and under the same rules as
those of the Great St. Bernard. Started in
1802, it remained unfinished till 1825, when
it was purchased by the St. Bernard Hospice.
We had some excellent *café au lait* here, and
a most interesting chat with an aged *réligieux*,
who took a great interest in our mounts.
He was very proud of having been deputed
to receive the Prince of Wales some years
ago when he visited the Great St. Bernard,
and was kind enough to show us all over
the Hospice, its accommodation for seventy
travellers and 150 workmen, its chapel, etc., etc.

He bade us a hearty " Au revoir," and we
started the descent of the Simplon.

The road immediately began to dip beyond
the Hospice, but the descent is so gradual we
hardly noticed it, except for the running away
which our bicycles seemed rather inclined to
do. We therefore kept just enough pressure on
the pedals to keep us going at a good pace,
without the very slightest exertion, along the
highest part of the Pass, which much resembles
the bed of a dried-up lake, and is bleak to a

From a Photo by G. Sommer & Figlio.

VILLAGE OF
SIMPLON.

89

degree. Soon after leaving the Old Hospice we came to the Seventh Refuge (5,855 ft.), and by the immense Rossboden Glacier to the village of Simplon (4,855 ft.). Most charmingly situated among pastures, it makes a delightful spot for a few days' stay at either of the two hotels of which it boasts. How very soon the surroundings changed as we descended from the heights of the Pass to the warmer regions! Instead of bleak, dreary rocks, at Simplon we were in the midst of pastures and luxuriantly green foliage, with mountain torrents rushing here and waterfalls there, tumbling down the mountain side. Each little stream seemed to be for ever anxious to join the larger brawling rivers away down in the valley, and the noise they all made was quite deafening, and entirely drowned the poor little "ting-tings" on the bells of our bicycles.

About half a mile lower down, the road, in forming a wide bend, entered the Laquin-Thal, after passing through the Gallery of Algaby. The loveliest part of the Pass, called the Ravine of Gondo, watered by the Doveria, now began.

This, without doubt, is one of the most sublimely grand gorges of the Alps, becoming narrower and deeper at every turn of the wheel, till at last its wet slate walls threatened to shut out the sky, and quite overhung the route.

Between the Eighth Refuge (3,841 ft.) and the Ninth Refuge (3,514 ft.) we crossed the Doveria by the Ponte Alto, and came to a huge mass of rock, which to all appearances blocked our

WATERFALL AT GONDO.

further progress. It is, however, tunnelled, or rather, pierced by the Gallery of Gondo of about 250 yards in length, the water dripping from

SIMPLON
ROAD.

From a Photo by G. Sommer & Figlio.

the roof as through an immense sieve. Just as we emerged at the further end of the gallery we came suddenly upon a magnificent waterfall, that makes the frail bridge by which it is crossed veritably tremble. In fact, there were countless cascades every few yards between here and Gondo, the last Swiss village, where we were stopped for Customs examination previous to entering Italy. Being already *plombés*, we had very little difficulty in getting through, which was such a pleasant surprise, we offered the officials a little refreshment, which they immediately accepted, leaving the Custom House to look after itself. We repaired to an attractive-looking "Osteria" and ordered some beer, and after having mutually drunk to one another's *bonnes santés*, mounted our bicycles and started off towards the Italian frontier. We hadn't gone more than half a mile, however, when it suddenly occurred to us that although we had offered the officials a drink, we had somehow or other forgotten to pay for it, and as it seemed too mean to let those poor fellows settle the score, we returned (much to their pleasure and genuine surprise) for that purpose.

After this little diversion we had a couple of miles' ride before we got to the Italian Custom

House, although we were in Italy soon after quitting Gondo.

It was close to Iselle (the Italian Customs), so history chronicles, that a thousand French troops who attempted to cross the Simplon from Switzerland were brought to a sudden stop, owing to a long bridge having been smashed to atoms by an avalanche (which are still very prevalent in this locality). As, however, the uprights of the bridge were still standing, a plucky soldier managed to get across from one to another, carrying with him a strong rope, which he made fast.

By this primitive contrivance the General, troops, and all their baggage were safely swung across the gorge and so entered Italy.

At Iselle we were not so fortunate in getting through, although, had we not lingered at Gondo, we should, I feel certain, have entered Italy without any duty being deposited on the machines during our stay in that country. The head official was out, and as the clerk in charge didn't seem to know much about his business, we essayed to get through by showing our C.T.C. tickets, and all but succeeded (in fact, the man had written out our passes), when the chief of the Customs came along, and then the fur began to fly. How those men

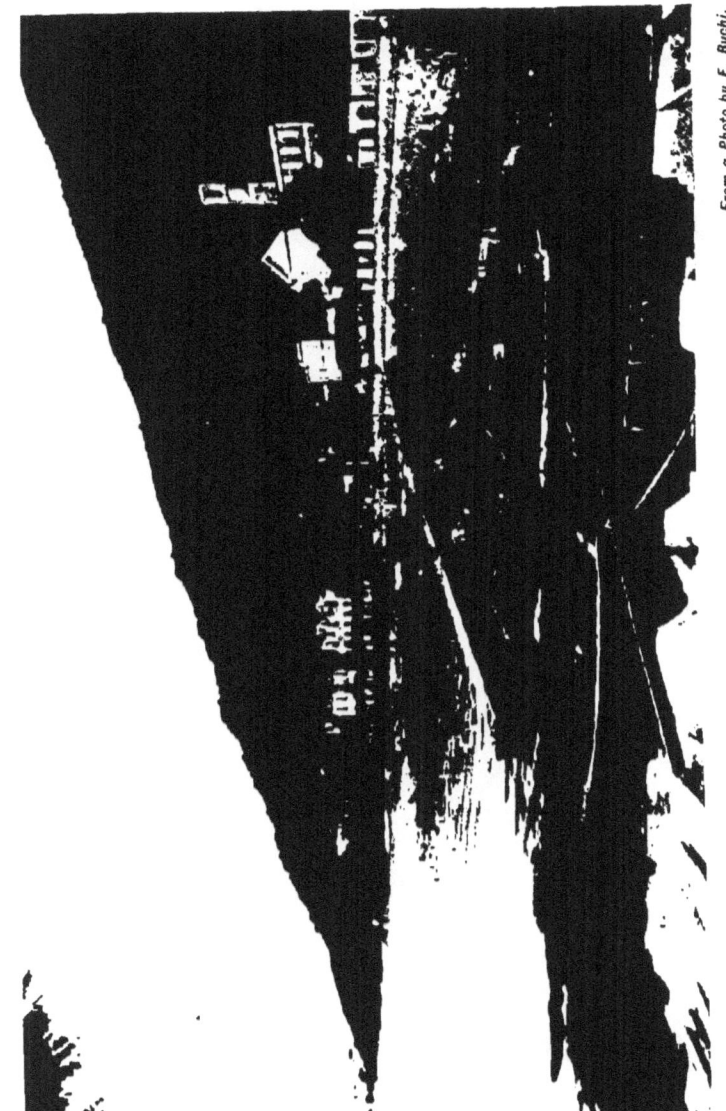

From a Photo by E. Buchi.

SUNA,
LAGO MAGGIORE.

1

did argue and jabber in Italian! and they got so heated in their discussion as to which of the couple was right, we were quite glad to deposit our fcs. 84, odd, and get on our way after being delayed nearly two hours. For some reason or other, a C.T.C. ticket does not give its owner a free entry into Italy, which deficiency could be easily remedied, I imagine.

The aforesaid chief showed me a list of cycle clubs who had made the request that all their *bonâ-fide* members showing their membership cards (and in some cases their photos) should be allowed a free pass into Italy, and said he had not the slightest doubt that if the C.T.C. made a similar request to the Italian Government it would be granted. Of course I don't believe it can be such a simple matter as merely writing and asking, or else surely such a useful and world-known institution as the C.T.C. would hàve arranged matters long ago for the benefit of its members.

However, we got off at last, and soon noticed a still further change in the vegetation and flora, which became more luxuriant at every turn of the road.

Figs, chestnuts, maize and mulberries all flourish in this graceful ravine, and there are vineyards galore a little further on at

Crevola (1,100 ft.), where for the last time we crossed the turbulent Doveria by a fine lofty bridge 100 ft. high, and entered the fertile Valle d'Ossola, which is exceedingly lovely and strikingly Italian in character, in spite of the frequent inundations which ravage this district. Not far from here we reached Domo d'Ossola, on the Tosa, where we again joined the railway, which has its terminus in this small town, and all passengers wishing to get into Switzerland from here must cross the Simplon by the magnificent route we had just left. I've done most of the Swiss Passes now on a bicycle, and must say I class the Simplon with my favorites, both for grandeur of scenery and the engineering skill displayed in the making of the roads.

Here we rested a couple of hours for our midday meal at the "Albergo della Corona Grossa."

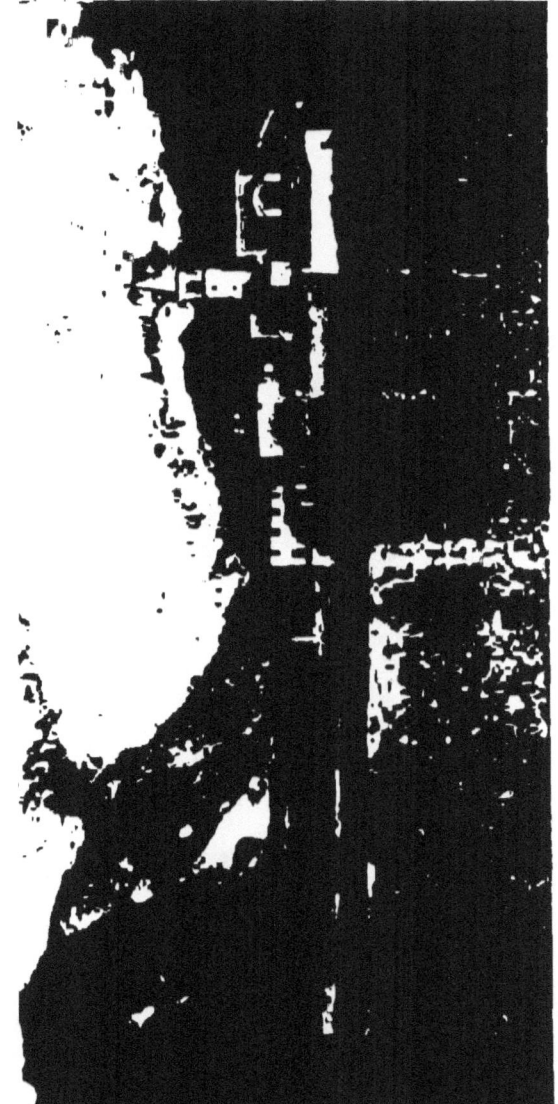

From a Photo by E. Buchi.

ISOLA PESCATORI,
LAGO MAGGIORE.

Chapter VIII.

WHAT a poverty-stricken place Domo d'Ossola seems to be! Every man, woman or child wants to show you the way, or do something (or nothing for preference) to earn a few sous.

And wasn't it hot here at Domo d'Ossola (905 ft.)? An Italian blue sky with not a cloud to be seen in any direction, it was a great contrast to the previous day's and night's soaking. If anything, we found it too warm for riding, and were very thankful to have our "Dr. Jims," as we nicknamed the large felt hats we wore. They are most comfortable and keep the sun off one's neck, as well as effectually shading the face. Then again, they can be bent to any shape the wearer pleases, and in bad weather rolled up and put in one's pocket to give place to the more conventional cap.

We left Domo d'Ossola by the main street, a typical one of an Italian village, with wide slabs of granite paving running in two parallel lines down the centre, and on which it is more pleasant to ride than on the veritable *pavé* (the bane of cyclists) on either side.

Soon after leaving the outskirts of the place

by way of a long avenue, we came to another perfectly straight road to Villa, following down the Toce river, which got wider and swifter the further we went. A grand road through groves of olive and walnut trees runs all the way through to Pallanzeno, there being scarcely a person to be seen in the heat of the day, when, as they say in Italy, only "dogs, fools and Englishmen are about." We were much astonished by the huge loads of hay stacked up on women's backs. In the distance these objects have the appearance of walking haystacks, but on closer inspection one finds a woman, generally old and decrepid, with this enormous load high up on her shoulders, trudging along contentedly enough. At Pallanzeno we branched off to the right to Piedimulera (800 ft.), which is at the entrance to the pretty Val'Anzasca, at the further end of which there are some gold mines of Pestarena, situated at the foot of Monte Rosa. I had arranged to meet an old school chum at Piedimulera, but owing to worse weather than we had anticipated it was my misfortune, after coming all this distance, to just miss him by a few hours, and only to find a letter from him awaiting me. The worst of it was we couldn't make ourselves understood

From a Photo by E. Buchi.

BORROMEAN ISLANDS,
LAGO MAGGIORE.

at all in these parts, with the result that we got hopelessly lost amongst vineyards and tall grass. We wandered about for nearly two hours in the direction we knew we ought to take, and found it very tiring work in the blazing sun, pushing heavily laden bicycles through fields of grass, every now and then one of us disappearing, bicycle and all, in a ditch. It was during one of these unpremeditated vanishings that I grazed my shin from instep to knee, on the same leg as I was bitten last year by a dog. This misfortune called forth from my companion the query, "Which was worst, the 'bark' or the 'bite'?" After that I thought we had indeed better find the high road, or disasters were bound to ensue; and at last we got to the river—but on the wrong side of it!

This was annoying, to say the least, as we could see the level highway just the other side of that swiftly flowing torrent. We had already forded half a dozen smaller streams, but this one was too broad and deep to tackle, so there was nothing for it but to follow down its banks till we came to some bridge or other. Patience was at length rewarded by a railway bridge hoving in sight.

This was a long way off too, and when we

did reach it the guard of the station close by absolutely forbade us to cross the bridge, although there was no train either way for at least six hours.

Entreaties were in vain, but a small bribe altered his opinion, and more than that, he consented to see us safely across, when at length we got on the high road again, after wasting three hours and a half in useless wanderings, and only having traversed something like four miles from Piedimulera.

PALLANZA.

"All's well that ends well," though, and once again · on the *grande route* we forgot our troubles, and spun along merrily through

CANNOBBIO.
LAGO MAGGIORE.

Cuzzago and Mergozzo, where we came to the pretty little lake of that name. All along from here to Pallanza (640 ft.), where we had arranged to stop the night, the telegraph posts are made of solid blocks of granite from fourteen to eighteen feet in height ; in fact, granite seems to entirely take the place of wood—fences, palings, posts, etc., are all granite, of which stone immense quarries abound in this locality. Suna is almost in Pallanza (which is on a promontory opposite to the Borromean Islands), and where we stayed at the Hôtel della Posta, right on the quay from which the steamboats start, and found it exceedingly comfortable too.

Chapter IX.

PALLANZA is a charming place, and a visit to the three islands of Pescatori, Bella, and Madre is well worth the row across the lake

PIAZZA DEL PROGRESSO, PALLANZA.

even on the very hottest day (especially if the boatman does the pulling). On the Isola Bella there are the most beautiful gardens imaginable, rising by ten terraces 100 feet above the level of the lake, and giving a sample of all the wealth of the luxuriant vegetation

From a Photo by E. Buchi.

BRISSAGO,
LAGO MAGGIORE.

113

of Italy — lemon and orange trees, cedars, magnolias, cypresses, laurels, camellias, etc., thrive. To my mind they are greatly disfigured by the shell grottoes, mosaics, and

PALLANZA.

dry fountains, but on the whole make a fine and many-tinted picture not easily forgotten.

A good night's rest and an excellent breakfast next morning, which was hotter than ever (the weather, not the breakfast), quite refreshed us after our previous day's hard work, and we strolled through this pretty old town taking numerous photos. One, of a crowd of market women, peasants and others round our mounts just previous to

PALLANZA.

embarking on the steamer for Locarno, was, I am sorry to say, a dismal failure owing to a too hasty snap-shot, in which nothing moved but the camera and operator (myself). From Pallanza we thought a trip up the lake by steamer would be delightful, and our anticipations proved correct, as besides having a more extensive view of this lovely Lago Maggiore than one could get at best riding along one side of the lake, we met some most interesting fellow travellers on board, the conversation

From a Photo by E. Buchi.

LUINO,
LAGO MAGGIORE.

opening by their enquiry as to whether we were two of Dr. Jameson's men? (We got rather tired of this question after a time.)

First, straight across the lake to Laveno and then backwards and forwards to Intra and Luino (the Italian Custom House), and a most impoverished place. Had it not been for the kind (though probably not disinterested) services of the waiter on board (he had been

FROM THE STEAMER ON LAGO MAGGIORE.

formerly for twelve years at Pagani's restaurant in London, and therefore knew English quite fluently), we might be at Luino still. We had been admiring from the deck of the steamer the loveliness of the banks of the lake, dotted with innumerable dwellings of all sorts and sizes, and surrounded by the most plenteous vegetation, consisting of chestnuts, vines, olives, figs, etc., when we were awakened from our day dreams by the aforesaid waiter. He intimated that if we wanted the deposit on our bicycles returned (which we had paid at Iselle), we should have to disembark at Luino for that purpose, bicycles and all.

Now this was a difficult matter, considering the boat was advertised to stop only three minutes at the place, which is scarcely sufficient

TORPEDO BOAT.

From a Photo by E. Buchi.

LOCARNO.
MARKET PLACE.

in which to find the Custom House, much less to get our money back, but here our waiter again aided us, as being on most friendly terms with *il capitano*, this official volunteered to wait for us till we had been through the douane. And, so as not to abuse his courtesy, as soon as we stopped at Luino, off we rushed trying in vain to closely follow the quickly retreating form of the *garçon*. We managed, however, to keep him in sight, but only by carefully watching the pair of white-stockinged and green-slippered feet which belonged to this obliging person.

Well, arrived at the Custom House, and presenting our papers was mere child's play ; but just think of it ! Fcs. 84, in gold or silver, was about eight times as much as the huge iron-bound coffers, presided over by the fierce-looking comptroller of the *dogana*, contained, so here was another hindrance. All he could manage was about 12 fcs. in coppers and 1 lire notes ; and *he* looked perplexed to a degree, while *we* were beginning to think we should either lose our money or the boat, when, Eureka ! the waiter once more came to our assistance. He happened to have about 70 francs on the steamer, which he offered to lend the Italian Government ; so off we bundled back to the landing stage and on to the boat, where we at last saw the colour of our money deposited at Iselle.

All this caused great amusement on board, and often have we laughed over the paupered

TORPEDO BOAT.

condition of Luino and the timely aid of the steamboat waiter.

Just off Cannobbio (one of the oldest places on the lake), I took photos of two of the

LOCARNO.
THE CASTLE.

From a Photo by E. Buchi.

small torpedo boats that ply on this lake to prevent smuggling, or at least to help minimise it. They are miniature torpedo boats, have search lights on board, and are moreover very fast and silent. Last Autumn (I think it

LOCARNO HARBOUR.

was) one of them was blown clean out of the water, and as all the crew were lost, the reason for this disaster could only be surmised, the supposition being that the boiler had burst, as boilers will do even on the best regulated Italian lake torpedo boats. This was probably the correct elucidation of the accident.

Just before arriving at Locarno, at the northern end of the lake, a sharp thunderstorm broke over us, followed by torrents of rain, and later by a most glorious sunset and a rainbow such as I have never seen before. One could quite easily trace the colours from edge to edge—red, orange, yellow, green, blue, indigo and violet. It was market day, too, at Locarno, with all the peasants in Cantonal costume. We weren't over comfortable where we stayed for the night, so I shall not mention the name of our hotel, as there are so many excellent ones.

Locarno (680 ft.), whose population of 3,500 is Roman Catholic, although a Swiss town, is thoroughly Italian in character, and it is most beautifully situated at the mouth of the Maggia. As we were informed that the early morning light was the best in which to see the grand view from the Madonna del Sasso, we climbed up to this church about 4 o'clock the morning after our arrival, and enjoyed immensely the fine survey it commands. As mass was in progress, we only just went inside to catch a glimpse of the "Entombment" of Ciseri and another picture by Bramantino, both very finely painted. A visit to the Val Maggia should not be missed if one has time, as it is one of the most

From a Photo by E. Buchi

LOCARNO.

picturesque (or "pictures-kew," as I heard it pronounced by an American) of valleys, with its bold and rugged rocky scenery, its richly fertile vegetation, and its numerous grand waterfalls for the whole of its length of 25 miles.

I don't know whether it was spite or not on the part of our informant, but he certainly didn't put us on the right road for Bellinzona when we left Locarno, and we found ourselves

BELLINZONA.

E 2

on a very wet pathway close to the lake's edge; in fact, at times the water encroached on to the "highway." After struggling and splashing along for some time, we met an old man who showed us where the high road was, so we carried our bicycles up the bed of a nearly dried-up river for about 300 yards and struck the correct route. Right along the 16 miles to Bellinzona the road mounts very slightly, but it was grand going and we speedily made up lost time and ran through Bellinzona to the "Café de la Gare" for breakfast. We took a photo from here of the several castles perched on hills on the east and west of this charming busy little town, where of late years the Swiss Federal Government has spent large sums in improving its natural fortifications.

LOCARNO.
MADONNA DEL SASSO.

From a Photo by E. Buchi.

Chapter X.

FROM Bellinzona to Flüelen on the Uri branch of the Lake of Lucerne it is about 95 miles by road over the St. Gothard Pass, and although from Biasca it mounts nearly all the way to the summit of the Pass (6,935 ft.), the ascent proper beginning soon after Airolo (3,755 ft.), I recommend this route most heartily as one of the finest to be seen in Switzerland from a bicycle. Besides being able to study the wonderful turnings and twistings of the St. Gothard Railway through its circular tunnels (I don't mean you can actually see the trains in the tunnels, because that is of course absurd), you have the superabundant flora of the Italian part of Switzerland, with vineyards, walnut trees, etc., to admire. These gradually became less noticeable, and at last, as we neared the summit, gave place to the scanty vegetation and bleak rocky scenery of the higher Alps. The skilfully engineered roads on this Pass appeared to me quite as striking as those on the Simplon.

On leaving Bellinzona we started almost due north for the first twelve miles or so, the road keeping on the east side of the valley; and very hot and dusty we found it, though exceedingly pretty, with the verdant pastures on the slopes on both sides watered by numerous cascades and streams which cross the road at intervals.

We were naturally obliged to ford them, which was pleasant enough in this hot weather. After passing through Osogna we still noticed the rich vines, mulberries, walnuts, and fig trees, but which gradually became scarcer as we went farther north. We especially remarked the manner in which the vines extend their dense foliage on wooden trellis-work, supported by granite pillars, in order that the bunches of grapes catch every ray of sunshine. And so on to Giornico, between which village and Faido (2,485 ft.) are the corkscrew tunnels of the railway. From the road we could easily trace the course of the line, and we watched a train enter the Travi Loop tunnel of nearly a mile in length, emerge, cross the Travi viaduct, then enter and leave the Pianotondo Loop tunnel, traverse the viaduct of the same name, and go through lastly, La Lume Tunnel — most interesting to see. As we pushed our bicycles up the Biaschina ravine, along the Ticino river, we marvelled exceed-

From a Photo by E. Buchi.

137

ingly on the nineteenth century's engineering skill, so well displayed on this important railway. It was near by, in December, 1478, a few hundred Swiss completely routed the Milan troops, by rolling down huge masses of rock from the mountain sides, and the engagement is still spoken of by the Tessin people as the " Battle of the Big Stones." Still ascending through richly wooded scenery, we came to Faido, and shortly after saw the same train enter the last loop tunnel on the Italian side, and called the Prato, about a mile in length. At the hamlet of Mairengo, close here, sprang the family of Delmonico, the well-known restaurateurs of New York.

Above Dazio Grande, the Ticino river has forced its way through the barrier of rocks, and noisily descends by magnificent leaps through this wild and rocky gorge. As we reached Airolo (the southern end of the famous St. Gothard Tunnel), the surroundings became more and more alpine, and we noticed especially the fine Pizzo Rotondo group to our left.

The present buildings of Airolo are quite modern, the village having been almost entirely destroyed by fire in 1877.

At 'the Hôtel de la Poste we were very comfortably housed for the night, previous to climbing the stiffer part of the route. It took us about three hours to the summit of the Pass (6,935 ft.), (*vid* the Val Tremola), where we found plenty of snow on either side of the road, and the usual small mountain lakes, and then began our descent to Hospenthal (4,800 ft.). Shortly before reaching this place, one has a most extensive and magnificent view. The Urseren Thal, which is the name of the valley, extends to the Furka Pass on the west, and the Oberalp Pass on the east. We followed the latter route for a mile or two to Andermatt, observing the imposing glacier of St. Anna high above the brow of the mountain to our right.

From Andermatt, over the Oberalp, and down the valley to Coire, is a most splendid route, and one I have ridden on a former occasion, though in an opposite direction, and makes a nice way of entering the Engadine on a bicycle by the Schyn Pass to Tiefenkasten, and thence by either the Julier or Albula Passes, the latter for preference, as regards scenery. We, however, continued the descent northwards, through the sombre Urner Loch (4,642 ft.), a tunnel seventy yards in length, driven through the rock, and then to the Devil's Bridge, where the Reuss river falls

NEAR LOCARNO.
BRIDGE ACROSS THE ISORNO.

From a Photo by E. Buchi.

into an abyss 100 feet below, wetting the bridge with its spray. The scenery here is wild in the extreme, and lends colour to the many legends which one hears from the natives about the " Teufelsbrücke."

Now descending by numerous windings the road traverses the dark rocky defile of the " Schöllenen " to Goeschenen, the northern station of the St. Gothard Tunnel. The tunnel was begun on June 4th, 1872, at Goeschenen, and a month later at Airolo, and from then until its completion on 29th February, 1880, an average of 2,500 men were employed on this huge work. The highest point of the tunnel (as it is also the highest point of the railway) is about half-way through, the time occupied in transit varying from 17 to 20 minutes.

Its construction cost sixty million francs, or £2,400,000 sterling, and it is stated that more than two million pounds weight of dynamite were used for blasting purposes in its structure.

What a difference there is in architecture, costumes, and even the physiognomy of the people between one end of this tunnel (9¼ miles in length) and the other! The ride down from Göeschenen to Flüelen is no less pleasing than the ascent to Airolo from

Bellinzona, and we were greatly captivated by the entrancing scenery, the going and the bold construction of the line, especially round Wasen.

There are some more circular tunnels, wonderful bridges, and a most bewildering succession of wild scraps of landscape. Feathery snow-white cascades leaping from the summits of lofty crags and falling hundreds of feet below, meet the eye in every direction. It is a magnificent road all the way down, but before we had gone very far on our journey we were obliged to replace our large felt hats by ordinary caps, owing to the strong wind blowing up the valley. It was bad enough standing still, but when we began to ride we had to pedal hard in spite of the gradual descent the whole way to Flüelen, a distance of about 26 miles. Leaving the village of Goeschenen, merrily we rode on through Wasen (3,055 ft.), from where we had a fine survey of the bold structure of the railway. Between here and Amsteg (1,760 ft.) at the foot of the Bristenstock, we on the road certainly had the advantage of those travelling by train, and it was really a most interesting and enjoyable ride in spite of the gale that was blowing.

As we neared the Lac des Quatres Cantons

FAIDO.
FALL OF PIUMORGNA.

From a Photo by G. Sommer & Figlio.

the gorge widens out to a valley, and instead of spinning along giddy precipices and over bridges from which we looked down upon ravines and tree tops, we were riding quietly along the straight road between Amsteg,* or, more correctly, "An den Stegen" (at the foot bridges), and Erstfeld, with the mountains looming up behind us like an army of snow-capped giants, who had been outpaced by the wheel. And now as we left the Gothard's fastnesses the wind dropped, and hurrying along the last few miles to Flüelen we just escaped a drenching thunderstorm that fortunately did not last long. It is at Altdorf (a couple of miles before we reached the lake) that tradition fixes the famous apple scene between Tell and Gessler. We had decided to take the steamer down the lake to Gersau, as to my mind it is by far the best and most pleasant way of seeing the Uri branch of the fascinating Vierwaldstättersee.

We soon came to the renowned Tellsplatte, where Tell sprang from his captors' boat, and which one cannot see from the Axenstrasse—that magnificent *diligence* road high up above

---

* Derives its name from the fact that there are two bridges here; one over the Reuss and the other across the Kerstelen-bach, a turbulent mountain torrent, from the "Hüfi Glacier," that rushes madly down to join the river.

the lake of Uri, and which is driven through the crags in several places—or from the railway. Then on the other side, just opposite Brunnen, is the " Mythenstein " or "Schiller's Rock," and just as one thinks the lake is shut in here by the mountains, it branches off to the west, and we come to still more enchanting scenery. At Gersau we disembarked, and rode thence by the route that follows the edge of the lake to Vitznau and Weggis. Gersau has often been styled the Swiss Nice, on account of the almost Italian climate it enjoys, owing to its sheltered position, which only allows the warm winds to blow over the place. Besides being able to enjoy a grand view of the lake and mountains from a point between Gersau and Vitznau, we had a good road, and caught the same steamer at Weggis to convey us to Lucerne. All along this delightful route we were surprised at the quantity of fig trees lining the highway, their luscious fruit looking very tempting. We met an officer on board who had been in India for thirty years, and was on his way home by the Overland Route. He evinced great interest in our ride, and wanted to hear all about the machines which had carried us safely so far, and said he would certainly become a votary of the wheel as

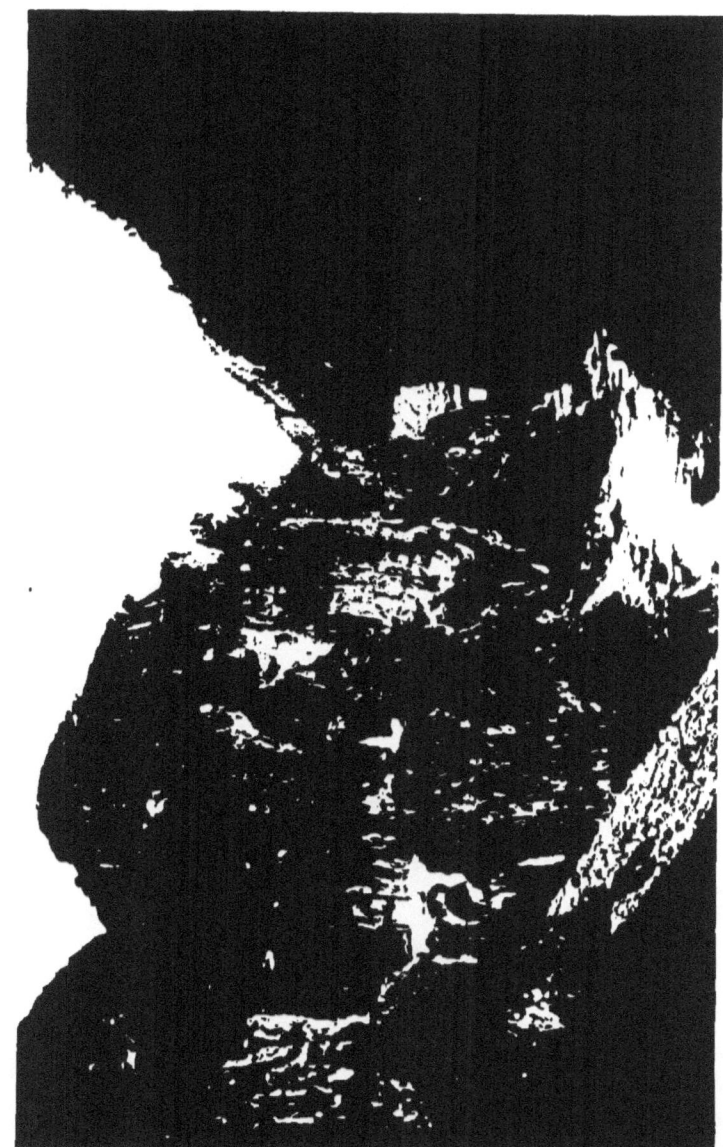

From a Photo by G. Sommer & Figlio.

AIROLO.

soon as he got home to England. It was also during our trip down this lake that an American·(whom I had met before, and who was not very *au fait* at French), asked me if I would act as his "interrupter." I mention this, not out of conceit, but merely because I think that his conception of the word gives one such an excellent idea of the general run of interpreters.

We soon came in sight of Lucerne, that most attractive of towns, located as it is in the very heart of Switzerland, which no one can claim to know unless he has spent a part of a summer in this lovely spot. In about the year 735, we are told, this large and thriving town consisted of a few fishermen's huts, while it now numbers 25,000 inhabitants.

Chapter XI.

So many guide-books to Lucerne and its environs have been published, and the place is so well known, I need hardly attempt to add anything about the town, which we did not make our resting place, pushing on to a small suburb named Emmenbrücke, where I have stayed many times before. There is an inn here, to which one comes (shortly after crossing a very long covered-in wooden bridge), where one is made as com-

OLD BRIDGE AT EMMENBRÜCKE.

OLD BRIDGE AT EMMENBRÜCKE.

fortable as one could wish, with but little
outlay, and where on this occasion we stayed
the best part of a week, taking sundry excursions on bicycle, boat and foot. A lovely trip
to make from here is to go by steamer to
Alpnach, and then ride by the lakes of Sarnen
and Lungern over the Brünig Pass (which
road is comparable only to a cinder track),
when one has the choice of two other fine
routes. Either through Meiringen over the

Grimsel Pass (which was opened only in 1895 to vehicular traffic) to the Rhone Glacier, etc., or through Brienz to. Interlaken for the Bernese Oberland, Thun, and Berne, and thence one can return *via* the Emmenthal to Lucerne.

Both of these are fine tours, and comprise the most sublime scenery one can well wish to see ; but there ! one can't go wrong in that respect in Switzerland. But to return to Emmenbrücke, which is the first station on the main line between Lucerne and Bâle.

We had a very enjoyable stay at this most modern inn, which flourishes under the name of "Hôtel Emmenbaum," and were fortunate enough to witness (even if we understood it not) a musical play in *patois*, which was acted entirely by the surrounding peasants, and wonderfully well done it was, considering the *dramatis personæ* the stage manager had at his disposal.

It was really very funny, and I wouldn't have missed it for anything. To begin with, the costumes were about as incongruous as one could imagine—a bright green and black satin riding habit doing duty for a duchess's gown, while the get-up of a supposed Englishman was too ludicrous. Green veil, blue goggles, bright red whiskers, white helmet, frock coat,

From a Photo by G. Sommer & Figlio.

SOUTHERN ENTRANCE TO
ST. GOTHARD TUNNEL,
AIROLO.

155

black gloves, white duck trousers, and top boots going to represent an English tourist on the top of a mountain ; but why they made him carry several knapsacks, a butterfly net and alpenstock, I couldn't understand. The audience (with the exception of ourselves), composed entirely of peasants, were delighted with our evident amusement of the whole thing, and vied with each other as to which of them should stand us (what turned out to be) a most unpalatable drink. The chief male lead was taken by the Hayden Coffin of the district—the village schoolmaster to wit—and besides his part, he obliged, when not otherwise engaged, by conducting the orchestra, who played in their shirt sleeves. Notwithstanding that they started the overture with their coats on, these were very shortly discarded, presumably to keep as cool as possible, as it certainly was a very sultry evening.

The following is a short sketch of the play. On the curtain rising we had a chorus of men and maidens, then the aforesaid village school-master gave forth a long discourse in *patois*, the chorus in the meantime turning their backs on the audience, evidently to show off to admiring relations the rest of their costumes.

On turning round, in a very shamefaced way, the chorus again sing.

In the meantime orchestra talk indiscriminately to audience and actors. Adolphus (amongst the audience) orders another bottle of red wine, and looks for approval to Angelina, who smiles. Chorus of men and maidens. Curtain.

Schoolmaster again. Chorus sit down. Enter haymakers. Then a Frenchman, his wife and a guide. Exeunt. In turn there come on Italians,

EMMENBRÜCKE.

a German student, a Jew pedlar (not a bicyclist), and a cowboy. Chorus rise and sing. Schoolmaster once more. Then the stationmaster's

From a Photo by the Photoglob Co.

GERSAU.
LAKE OF LUCERNE.

red-headed sister (this sounds like Ollendorf) obliges with a solo—very flat.

Several exceedingly well executed glees and ——. Curtain.

The setting of the play was supposed to represent a mountain trip, each scene being higher up the mountain than the preceding one.

I must candidly admit that the choruses were in perfect harmony, and if we could have understood one word of the *patois* we should no doubt have appreciated their efforts even more. Otherwise the native talent was not great.

It was during one of our rides round Lucerne that going through a narrow village street we came to several cows blocking the way. X passed by them safely, but the last cow, evidently rather astonished, suddenly turned broadside on to me, with the result I went straight into her ribs, which necessitated a hurried dismount.

Excepting a plaintive " moo," she didn't seem to object to this sudden invasion, but turned complacently round, leaving me to remount and ride after my friend, who had not noticed the incident.

Chapter XII.

OUR next destination was Zürich, and I cannot conscientiously recommend the road as one of the best in Switzerland ; on the contrary, it was one of the worst *grandes routes* I have ridden in that country. The first part is rather good, and a nearly straight road takes one to Cham, on the Lake of Zug at its northern end, but it was not a very interesting ride to this village, which is chiefly noted for a large manufactory of condensed milk. However, soon after leaving Cham things got lively enough, and although the following incident may sound incredible, I am giving the exact facts of the case, as were sworn by my companion and myself before the Swiss Legation on our return to England about a week later.

We had just passed through Knonau when we had an exciting adventure, but luckily with no very dire results. We had been riding quite peacefully down a slight decline, admiring the undulating landscape and chatting, when just at the bottom of the hill we noticed a large hay-cart drawn across the road. As there wasn't room for us both to ride abreast, which we were in

From a Photo by G. Sommer & Figlio

BRÜNIG PASS

F 2

the habit of doing, I went first, X following me closely. I had only just passed the cart when without the slightest warning a peasant (who from behind the cart had evidently watched us approach) jumped out in a fuming mad rage and slashed me across the back with a huge stock-whip. My friend, riding directly after me and unable to pull up short, also came in for a cut on *his* shoulders. Although rather taken aback (in two senses of the word) at this sudden and unwarranted attack, we instantly jumped off our bicycles and went for him, X giving our assailant one or two very artistic slashes across his face with a small whip we each carried to keep dogs off our legs, and the coward immediately began to blubber and (I imagine) crave for mercy. I meantime was engaging another peasant, who (let me truthfully add) didn't show fight. A woman on the scene calling out loudly to other peasants for help, six or eight of them came running up with scythes and pitchforks, presumably to assist their friends. We thinking "discretion the better part of valour," and having settled our man, mounted our machines and made off sharp, a volley of stones starting us on our journey. One can hardly credit that on the high road of such a frequented part of

'Switzerland two harmless cyclists should be made the object of such an assault, but the foregoing account is the "honest, manly, sweet, straightforward, unadulterated truth" (as Hawtrey used to say).

As we were riding with our coats rolled up on the handle bars, owing to the great heat, we had simply a flannel shirt to lessen the force of the blow, with the result that each of us bore for some time after the mark of the thong of the stock-whip, in the shape of a blood-wheal 14 to 16 inches in length and about ½-inch wide, which *looked* very vicious for a day or two, and caused considerable pain and annoyance, especially at night. The man must have been mad, or perhaps had some grievance against cyclists, as there was absolutely no reason for him to attack us, and we, moreover, never saw him till he struck me. I have ridden thousands of miles in and around Switzerland, and have always, with this exception, found the natives more than willing to show me the road, or help in any little way that I might ask of them. The only reason I can suggest in this case is that a motor-car, which had passed a few minutes before, *may* have startled the peasants and their cattle, but as they (the peasants, *not* the cattle) only spoke an unin-

From a Photo by the Photoglob Co.

TONNEHALLE,
ZÜRICH.

telligible *patois*, and lots of it, we couldn't make out a single phrase. No doubt we should rightly have gone to the British Consul on arriving at Zürich, but we were most anxious "for fresh woods and pastures new," and to ride on to Constance next day. Being afraid we should be detained in Zürich to identify the man, we said nothing about it to the authorities till we got home to London, when we made a declaration at the Swiss Legation, as before stated. The British Consul at Zürich, to whom I sent the declaration, said he would do all in his power to have the man suitably punished if they could identify him, and I do not think any intending riders abroad need have the least fear that they would be attacked in a similar fashion.

After this little adventure we had a nice ride by Affoltern and Birmensdorf to Zürich, where we put up at the St. Gothard Hotel (near the station, and very comfortable). Zürich is a splendid city, and a prosperous one into the bargain, with a population of 110,000. There are a great many fine buildings to be seen, and notably the "Tonnehalle," situated close to the lake, where sweet music is discoursed the while one drinks a *choppe* of beer or dines *al fresco à la carte*.

Then there is the Uetliberg, a fine point of view, with its rugged mountain scenery, intruding as it does into the midst of a district which human industry has converted into one vast garden. A stroll through the town shows one most of the important buildings, and the best place to go, for any information required, is to the "Official Enquiry Office" in the Bahnhof Strasse.

At this office enquiries are answered free of charge, and in most of the larger towns in Switzerland there are similar information bureaux, where one can obtain gratis a small guide-book of the place.

SCHAFFHAUSEN.

From a Photo by the Photoglob Co.

Chapter XIII.

NEXT morning we started early, and had a fine ride to Winterthur, just outside which town my back tyre punctured very slightly. This was the one and only puncture either of us had in a ride of over 600 miles, which speaks volumes for the roads and the tyres; and as for the other three wheels, we never even used the inflator once. Winterthur (1,445 ft.) is an important manufacturing town, with a fine "Stadthaus," designed by Semper, and an excellent panorama of the Rigi, which are worth a visit. From Winterthur to Frauenfeld we were accompanied by several native cyclists, who didn't make a very hot pace, and seemed much inclined to walk their machines on the flat, as well as up a few small inclines.

We refreshed ourselves at Frauenfeld, and were much amused at a little dog belonging to the innkeeper. When we asked how much we owed for the wine the man mentioned the amount, and then asked us to throw the money on the floor, which we did. Immediately the little dog picked up the coins in his mouth, and trotted off to his master to deposit the

money in his hand. The animal, with the
sagacity of the canine race, wouldn't take the
money to anyone else, but, directly he heard
a coin fall on the floor, he grabbed it up and
took it to his master. Through Pfyn and
Lipperswil it is all uninteresting enough, undulating roads being the general thing, but shortly
after we had a slight descent into Constance (in
Germany), on entering which town we were
asked if we had anything to declare. On our
replying in the negative we were instantly
allowed to go on without any bother at all,
and riding through the town, put up for two
nights at the " Hôtel Krone," which we found
most comfortable and well situated. Karl
Kaysser is a competent repairer of bicycles
and thoroughly understands them ; he, however,
only speaks German, but I mention his name
in case some cyclist may find himself at Constance wanting some repairs effected, and I
can recommend him. Constance, or Konstanz
(1,335 ft.), is a military town of Baden, and
a dear old place it is, with many interesting
buildings and relics. The Insel Hotel, formerly
a Dominican monastery, is worth a visit,
besides being a well-conducted and cheerful
hotel to stay at. Then one shouldn't miss
seeing the Cathedral, founded in 1052, with

From a Photo by the Photoglob Co

FALLS OF
THE RHINE

its open spire, from which one gets an admirable survey of the surrounding country and lake. A walk through the streets of this old town offers a continual sight of picturesque architecture on account of the old buildings which abound. We strolled about, seeing the sundry places of interest, and went off to bed early as we had to be up betimes the following morning to catch the first boat for Lindau at the other end of the Lake of Constance. The morning was overcast and generally depressing, and as the day wore on, although there were promises of a finer afternoon, the weather didn't improve much, so that we had hardly any view at all, and were not greatly impressed by the beauty of the surroundings about which we had heard so much. The steamer put in at Meersburg (an antique town rising on terraces on the German side of the lake), Immenstaad, Friedrichschafen, Langenargen, and various other ports before getting to Lindau, where we disembarked. Several of these places have quite large harbours, and as there are Swiss, German and Austrian companies whose steamboats ply on this lake, there must be a considerable amount of navigation on the "Bodensee." At Lindau, in Germany still, we lunched at the "Bayerischer

Hof," and having finished our meal, thought a walk round this island town would be interesting. We hadn't gone very far, however, before some suspicious little puffs of wind and a leadeny sky, followed by a strange calm, seemed to indicate an approaching gale. It was the calm that precedes the storm, for hardly had we got back to the shelter of the hotel when, with a sudden rush, the tempest (for such it was) burst forth with all the demoniacal force of a hurricane. We could easily follow its course on the water, which in a very short time became a regular sea, with waves higher and bigger than I thought them possible on a lake.

I have often noticed in Switzerland the forerunners of a severe storm. The clouds grow denser and denser, taking all sorts of weird forms, and gradually creep to the summit of the mountains. If the sun has been shining, he seems to turn sickly and pale. At night the air is so oppressive and still, that not a leaf stirs, and should there be a moon visible, she has a large halo, while "falling stars" are seen in every direction. The far-away mountains appear suddenly to have come much closer, and even the animals seem to be aware of the change

From a Photo by the Photoglob Co.

LAUFENBURG.

179

about to take place in the elements. And
then the storm comes up with the Föhn wind
with a rush and a clatter through the valleys,
bringing terror in its wake. A severe storm
in the mountains is a sight to be remembered
for ever, and is naturally all the more imposing
and awe-inspiring by night.

To return to the tempest in question. Rain
in torrents, as well as the wind, knocked on
the head our proposed ride back on our
bicycles to Constance, and we returned as
we had come, by steamer. That was bad
enough, and we had a nice toss up into the
bargain. Waves were breaking over the bows
every minute, and several people who ventured
on deck got well drenched for their daring.
Some of the passengers were not good sailors,
I'm sorry to say, and altogether the trip
back was not one of unmixed pleasure and
enjoyment, so that by the time we disembarked
at Constance, after a long "battling with the
waves," we'd had quite enough Lake for one
day. It was a pity we missed the fine view
we should have had of the snow-clad ranges
of the Alps on the south-eastern horizon,
with a foreground of the forest of Bregenz,
and the green meadows of Appenzell.

I am told the Island of Mainau is well

worth a visit, and, as the guide-book says, "is the most lovely spot of the whole Lake of Constance, and of an idyllic beauty. A poetical charm seems to animate it, and splendid parks and gardens of a meridional character surround the beetling castle." Even this flowery language could not induce us to chance missing a view of the Falls of the Rhine on a moonlight night, so we pushed on next day in the direction of Schaffhausen.

From a Photo by the Photoglob Co.

LAUFENBURG.

183

Chapter XIV.

IN all my rides in Switzerland I've certainly never ridden on a better stretch of road than from Constance to the outskirts of Bâle, the going nearly the whole way of about 100 miles being as nearly perfect as possible.

Soon after starting · from Constance we crossed into Switzerland again, and rode on, most of the way following the Rhine down stream close to the water's edge, through Ermatingen and Steckborn. The river got narrower and more rapid as we rode through several small towns and villages, passing the pretty little town of Stein, with its remarkable old houses with painted façades. Here, too, in the "Klosterli" of St. George, are some highly interesting carved ceilings, wainscots, and mural decorations. Then on to Diessenhofen, where we cut off a curve in the river, and descending somewhat abruptly, crossed it by a long low bridge into Schaffhausen on the right bank. This town presents a most enchanting appearance when viewed from the village of Feuerthalen, through which we passed just before entering Schaffhausen, and which really forms part of it. We rode through it, and up a long tiring hill to Neuhausen, staying at the "Schweizerhof," right opposite the Falls of the Rhine. And what a splendid sight they are! The finest views of the Falls are, without doubt, to be had from the Schweizerhof Hotel and its extensive grounds. Soon after we got here and had had dinner, the illumination of the Falls with electric and Bengal lights began, a large rocket announcing the fact. We gazed in admiration at this entrancing sight, enhanced by the changing colours of the Bengal fires, and we listened to the roar of the Falls long after the illuminations had finished with a grand show of rockets. We were certainly well rewarded for waiting, for the moon rose in all her unequalled splendour, shedding her cold white light on the Falls and their surroundings, giving us an impression of the sublime, which, I am sure, will never fade from my memory. To view the Falls properly and thoroughly one must see them by night as well as by day, and I most strongly recommend a night or two spent at Neuhausen for this purpose. Owing to the great amount of rain and the melting snow, the river was much swollen, and we were told that not

RHEINFELDEN.

From a Photo by the Photoglob Co.

for years had the Falls been seen to such advantage, although in ordinary years they are in point of volume the grandest in Europe. If, reader, you are within cycling distance, do not miss one of the finest waterfalls to be seen anywhere. Taking the rapids and cataracts into consideration, the total height of the fall is about 100 feet, and seeing them before 8 a.m., as we did on the following day, countless numbers of rainbows, formed by the sunshine in the clouds of spray, added to the ravishing picture. Baedeker gives the best route to follow in order to see the Falls from all points of view, and it is extraordinary the varying aspects they have when seen from different spots. The " Rheinfall-Brücke " is also most interesting, its nine arches differing in span, owing to the difficulty in obtaining foundations for the piers.

Chapter XV.

WELL, we took a final fond look at the Falls, then started off on our last day's ride to Bâle, and shortly after quitting Neuhausen we crossed into Germany again. It is indeed very difficult, following the Rhine along here, to know when one is in Switzerland and when in Germany, as we did not notice any Custom Houses till we arrived at Laufenburg, where we crossed the Rhine for the last time by an extremely pretty bridge, and remained in "La Belle Suisse" till we ran into Bâle.

Soon after leaving Neuhausen we forsook the river for some time, and ascended gradually along a perfect road through Jestetten to Dettighofen, where the descent began and continued right away through Griesen and Thiengen to Waldshut, where we again met the Rhine. There are numerous small villages along both banks, but we kept on the German side for a few miles further till we arrived at Laufenburg, where, as before mentioned, we traversed the Rhine by an old bridge, and riding through the town put up for our mid-day meal at the " Hôtel Adler" near the river. This little Swiss town on the left bank is very prettily placed, its ruined castle, lofty church and old watch-towers overlooking the impetuous rapids (called the "Laufen") which the Rhine forms just here. From Laufenburg we followed the left bank, the road running through forests of pine trees right away to Sackingen, and then cutting off a bend of the river brought us safely to Rheinfelden. Here we again went under archways both on entering and leaving the town. These archways, which are very characteristic of the towns and villages here situated, impressed us both greatly.

Just as we were preparing to leave Rheinfelden, Jupiter Pluvius once more favoured us, and as it had been raining heavily most of the day between this town and Bâle, the last ten miles of our ride were very unpleasant. Naturally there is a great deal of heavy traffic to and from such an important place as Bâle, and the roads were inches deep in mud and well nigh impassable. In some places our driving wheels skidded along merrily for several yards, which generally occasioned a hasty and dirty dismount, and filled our shoes with liquid mud. In spite of this, we rode into the town without mishap, and remained for the night and next

191

day at the "Jura Hotel," so as to be near the station.

As can be seen by following our ride on the map, we almost went round Switzerland, though we were unable to make a complete circle as we had anticipated. The bad weather we experienced, and the lateness of the season, made it impossible to negotiate the Stelvio Pass as pre-arranged. Well, that will be for another time, and I am told by a gentleman who has walked it, that some of the finest scenery of the Alps is to be seen on this Pass, although I can't conceive anything grander than the Engadine and some of the higher passes of the Alps, such as the Gothard, Simplon, Furka, Grimsel, Oberalp, Maloja, etc.

Bâle, our goal, being reached in safety, we spent the next day in "doing" the sights of this thriving town and cleaning our bicycles, previous to bringing them back to London on the following evening. I had hoped to get, at Bâle, more photographs of places we had passed through since Constance, but there seems to be no sale for them here, as we were only able to obtain a very indifferent selection, which were not worth purchasing.

From Bâle a multitude of excursions can be made in the environs, which should afford the

greatest delight to the traveller who has a certain amount of time to spare either before going further south to the Alps or on his return. As we knew the surroundings by heart, and not having any extra time on our hands, we contented ourselves with a 36 hours' stay in this busy city, going over a large ribbon manufactory (of which there are many, and which we found most interesting), and taking a last long look at the Black Forest, the Jura and Vosges, previous to starting home to the "smoky village" of London. The Cathedral, with its parti-coloured roof, is worth a visit, and there are many buildings and places of interest, on which exhaustive guide-books are procurable at every bookseller. The caricatures of six of the leading personages of Bâle, by the celebrated painter Bocklin, can be seen on the keystones of the façade of the "Kunsthalle," and are most amusingly and cleverly designed. These grotesque representations caused considerable discussions as to whether they should be allowed to remain or not, after Bocklin had finished them, but the inhabitants insisted that there was no offence offered or given, and there they are to this day.

At Bâle our ride for 1896 came to an end, and during our stay in the land of the Switzers described as "a cluster of delights and grandeurs" by an American poet, we had ridden and pushed our bicycles very nearly 1,000 kilomètres, or about 620 English miles.

. A shorter article entitled "Cycling in the High Alps," an account of another tour we made in 1895, appeared in the June number of the *Badminton Magazine*, and I can think of no more pleasant way of spending a holiday ranging from three weeks to two months than by a combination trip of these two rides. The intending cyclist should certainly know French and a slight knowledge of German and Italian he would find most useful. Of course, riding in the "Plain" of Switzerland is not very arduous labour, but for the higher and more mountainous parts one must be prepared for a lot of hard work, and to "rough it" considerably at times.

In conclusion let me say, do not overdo it. One is so apt to think one is not a bit tired owing to the magnificent air! and certainly I've found I could always ride more in Switzerland in a day without any feeling of fatigue, than I ever could in England—but this may be fancy.

A little care in the distance one rides the